THE MAN IN THE MOON AND HIS FLYING BALLOON

Written and illustrated by LOU ALPERT

Whispering Coyote Press Inc./New York

Published by Whispering Coyote Press Inc.
P.O. Box 2159, Halesite, New York 11743-2159
Text copyright © 1991 by Lou Alpert
Illustrations copyright © 1991 by Lou Alpert
Printed in the United States of America
ISBN 1-879085-05-4

To Mom
with Love

As the moon appears
in the sky tonight,
I crawl to my window
to see the sights,

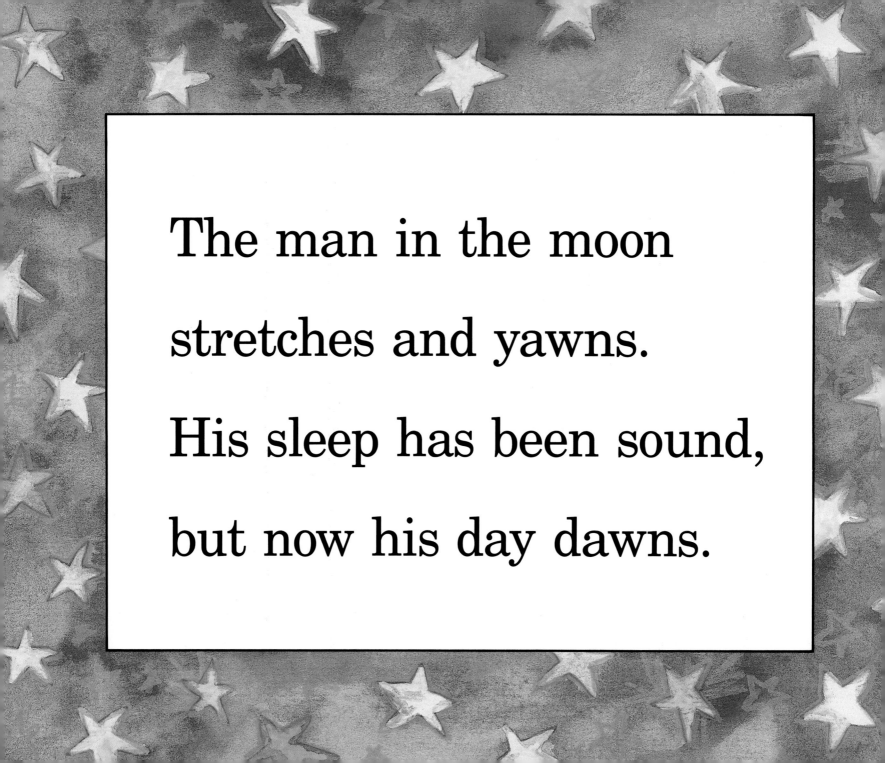

The man in the moon
stretches and yawns.
His sleep has been sound,
but now his day dawns.

And quickly
makes ready
his flying balloon.

He gathers the stars
before they wake,

Lifting them gently
with shovel and rake.

Loading them into

his flying balloon,

He heads for the sky

not a minute too soon.

Holding each star

in his loving fingers,

He brushes away

the sleep that lingers.

He places each star

in the sky as night falls,

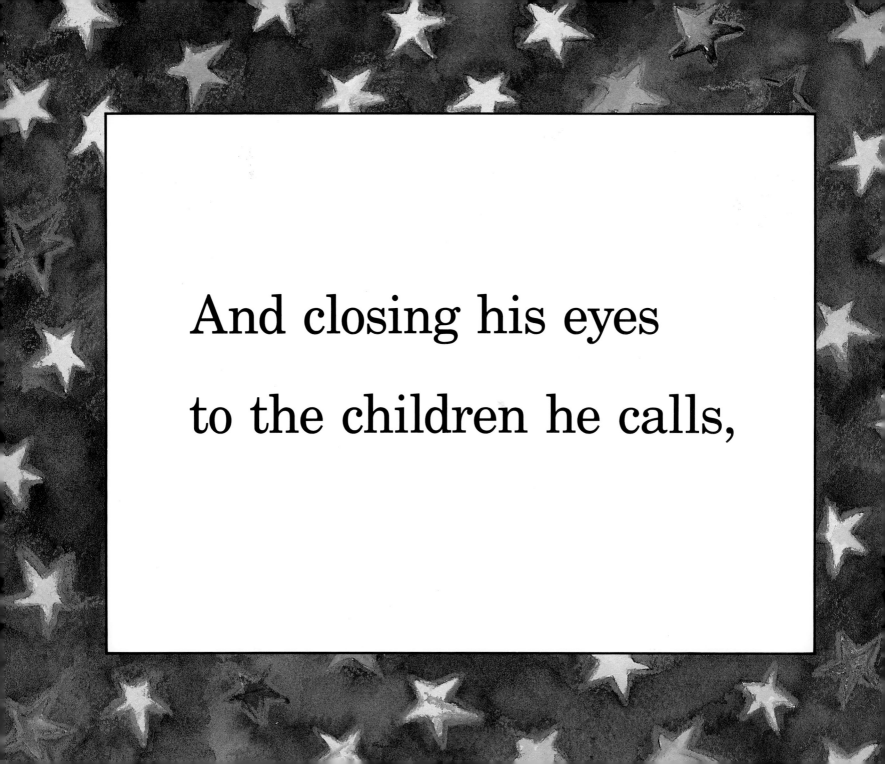

And closing his eyes

to the children he calls,

"Give me your thoughts
your wishes and dreams,
I'll light up the sky
with my magical beams."

Every child's wish brings a new star in sight. Showering the heavens with glittering light.

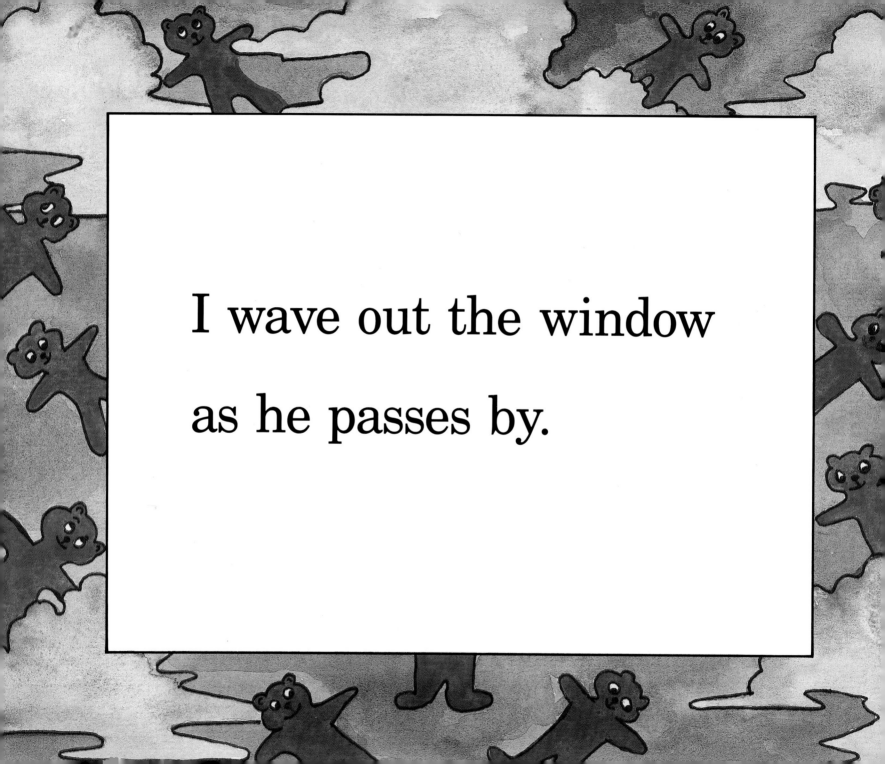

I wave out the window
as he passes by.

He tips his hat

and points to the sky.

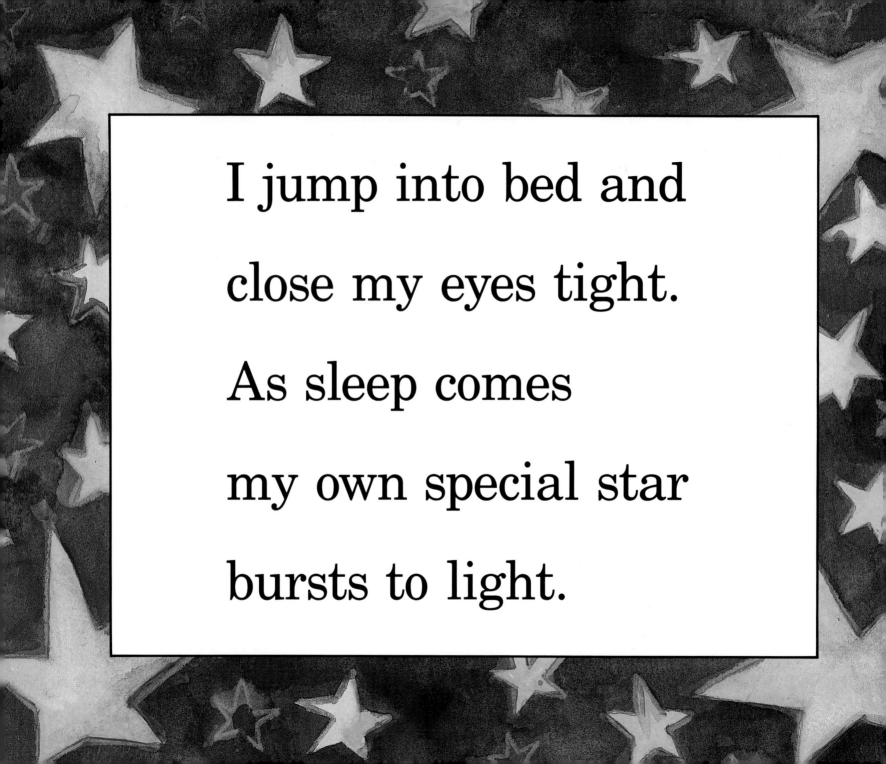

I jump into bed and

close my eyes tight.

As sleep comes

my own special star

bursts to light.